Dear Parents:

Congratulations! Your child is taking the first steps on an exciting journey. The destination? Independent reading.

STEP INTO READING® will help your child get there. The program offers five steps to reading success. Each step includes fun stories and colorful art or photographs. In addition to original fiction and books with favorite characters, there are Step into Reading Non-Fiction Readers, Phonics Readers and Boxed Sets, Sticker Readers, and Comic Readers—a complete literacy program with something to interest every child.

Learning to Read, Step by Step!

Ready to Read   Preschool–Kindergarten
• big type and easy words • rhyme and rhythm • picture clues
For children who know the alphabet and are eager to begin reading.

Reading with Help   Preschool–Grade 1
• basic vocabulary • short sentences • simple stories
For children who recognize familiar words and sound out new words with help.

Reading on Your Own   Grades 1–3
• engaging characters • easy-to-follow plots • popular topics
For children who are ready to read on their own.

Reading Paragraphs   Grades 2–3
• challenging vocabulary • short paragraphs • exciting stories
For newly independent readers who read simple sentences with confidence.

Ready for Chapters   Grades 2–4
• chapters • longer paragraphs • full-color art
For children who want to take the plunge into chapter books but still like colorful pictures.

STEP INTO READING® is designed to give every child a successful reading experience. The grade levels are only guides; children will progress through the steps at their own speed, developing confidence in their reading.

Remember, a lifetime love of reading starts with a single step!

Copyright © 2025 Disney Enterprises, Inc. All rights reserved. Published in the United States by Random House Children's Books, a division of Penguin Random House LLC, 1745 Broadway, New York, NY 10019, and in Canada by Penguin Random House Canada Limited, Toronto, in conjunction with Disney Enterprises, Inc.

Step into Reading, Random House, and the Random House colophon are registered trademarks of Penguin Random House LLC.

Visit us on the Web!
StepIntoReading.com
rhcbooks.com

Educators and librarians, for a variety of teaching tools, visit us at RHTeachersLibrarians.com

ISBN 978-0-7364-4515-3 (trade) — ISBN 978-0-7364-9053-5 (lib. bdg.)
ISBN 978-0-7364-4516-0 (ebook)

Printed in the United States of America

10 9 8 7 6 5 4 3 2 1

Random House Children's Books supports the First Amendment and celebrates the right to read.

STEP INTO READING®

Disney PRINCESS

MULAN and the LANTERN FESTIVAL

by Kimberly Lee
adapted by Nicole Johnson
illustrated by the Disney Storybook Art Team

Random House 🏠 New York

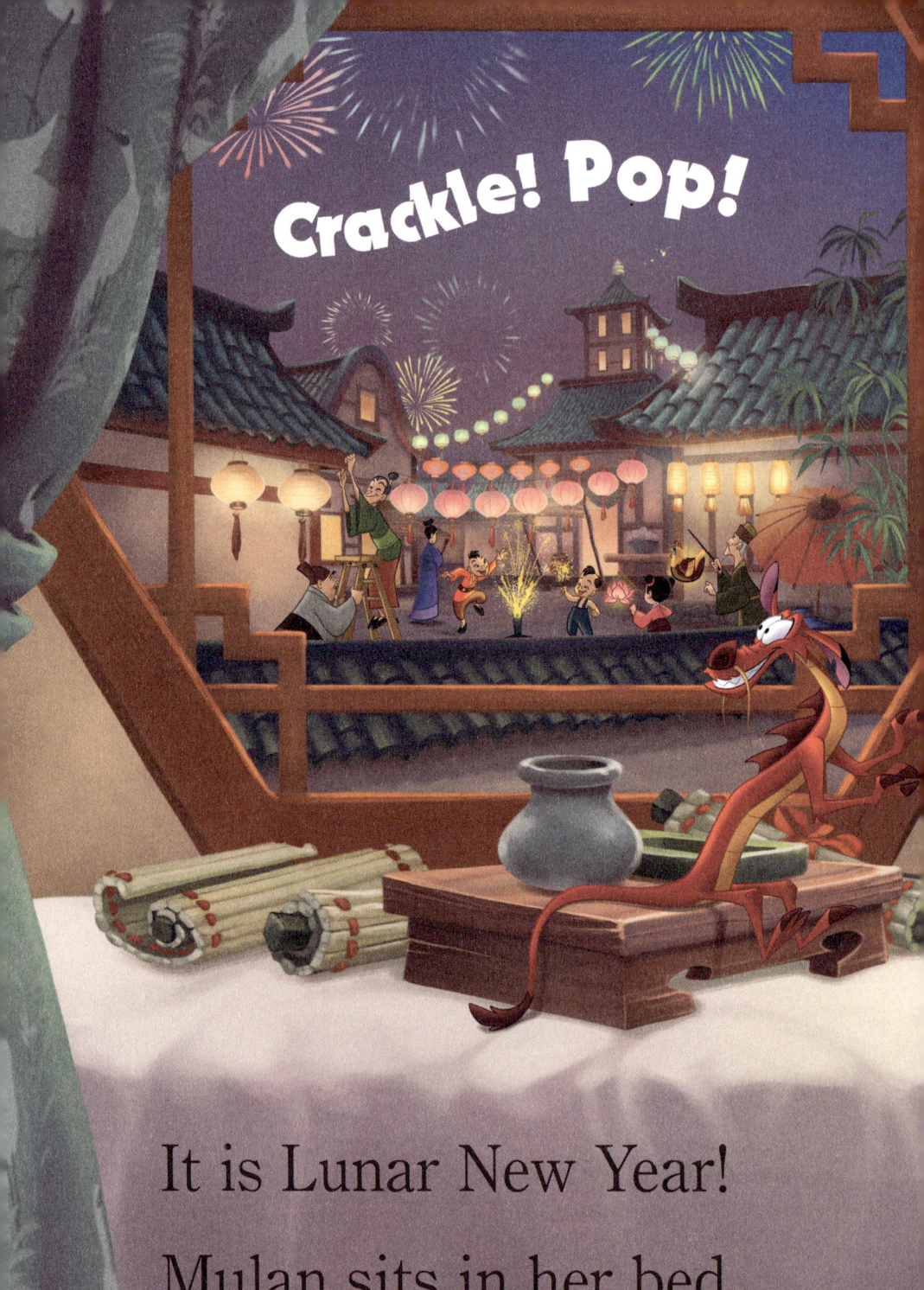

It is Lunar New Year!
Mulan sits in her bed.

She watches fireworks outside her window.

The Lantern Festival is happening soon! It is always on the last day of Lunar New Year.

Mulan shows Mushu and Cri-Kee her lantern. It is a dragon!

Mulan drops her lantern.

The lantern is torn!

Mulan is sad.

She leaves her room.

Grandmother Fa sees Mulan go.

She has an idea.

Mulan had made the lantern when she was a kid. Mulan decides that she will fix it!

But the lantern is not in her room!
A note is on her bed.
It says to go to the kitchen.

Mulan finds her parents in the kitchen.

They are eating dumplings.

The Fa family eats dumplings every year for Lunar New Year.

Mulan's father gives her a second note.

It says to look outside.

Mulan looks out a window.

She sees Khan

and Cri-Kee.

Khan has a lantern!

Mulan goes outside. She finds a note in the lantern. It says to look for the strongest ship.

Mulan goes to the river.

She sees lots of strong ships.

But none of them

has a note.

Mulan returns home.
She finds Grandmother Fa.

She has Mulan's torn lantern! The strongest ship is *frien*ship!

Grandmother Fa takes the notes. They can use the paper to fix the lantern!

Grandmother Fa and Mulan glue the notes to the tear in her lantern.

The lantern is fixed!
It is even better now because Grandmother Fa and Mulan fixed it together.

Mulan gives her
grandmother
a great big hug!

Mulan and her family
go to the festival.
The world is full
of love and light!
Happy Lunar New Year!